A PENG

THE GOLDBLUM ... NS

Helen McClory lives in Edinburgh and grew up between there and the Isle of Skye. Her debut novel, *Flesh of the Peach*, was published by Freight in spring 2017. Her first collection, *On the Edges of Vision*, won the Saltire First Book of the Year 2015 and was republished by 404 Ink in spring 2018. 404 Ink also published her newest collection, *Mayhem & Death*, in March 2018. There is a moor and a cold sea in her heart.

THE GOLDBLUM VARIATIONS

*Adventures of Jeff Goldblum Across the
Known (and Unknown) Universe*

HELEN McCLORY

PENGUIN BOOKS

PENGUIN BOOKS
An imprint of Penguin Random House LLC
penguinrandomhouse.com

First published in Great Britain by 404 Ink, 2018
This updated edition published in Penguin Books 2019

LIBRARY OF CONGRESS CATALOGING-IN-PUBLICATION DATA

Names: McClory, Helen, author.
Title: The Goldblum variations / Helen McClory.
Description: New York : Penguin Books, [2019] |
Identifiers: LCCN 2019027122 (print) | LCCN 2019027123 (ebook) |
    ISBN 9780143135227 (trade paperback) |
    ISBN 9780525506898 (epub)
Subjects: LCSH: Goldblum, Jeff, 1952—Humor.
Classification: LCC PN2287.G5785 M33 2019 (print) |
    LCC PN2287.G5785 (ebook) | DDC 791.4302/8092—dc23
LC record available at https://lccn.loc.gov/2019027122
LC ebook record available at https://lccn.loc.gov/2019027123

Printed in the United States of America
10 9 8 7 6 5 4 3 2 1

Set in Berling LT Std
Designed by Sabrina Bowers

Contents

THE
GOLDBLUM
VARIATIONS

A Variety of Jeff Goldblums

The Jeff Goldblum that lathes and sands down a pine table, brushing the grain with the heel of his hand, bends down and takes a spirit level to it, saying gently to the wood, *well done, you*.

⸙

The Jeff Goldblum that wakes up in the morning, opens the curtains and says, softly, "Oh!"

⸙

The Jeff Goldblum that, in an excitable mood, makes his maid an origami peacock and leaves it on the top of the fridge (where she, being short, cannot reach it without his helpful boost).

The Jeff Goldblum that has never forgotten your birthday, having chanced upon it in the Wikipedia article about you, which he has started to contribute to, although he doesn't really know anything about you at all, and, while his contributions are always peevishly removed by moderators, he is only writing kind and harmless things, like saying your favorite color is pink, when, citation needed, it might not be so, though it might be, because he, Jeff Goldblum, has surmised a favorability toward pinkness in you, stranger.

The Jeff Goldblum that lets tears flow when he dead-heads his roses in winter.

The Jeff Goldblum that is reading these stories with his chin in his hands.

The Jeff Goldblum that is reading these stories with his head in his hands.

The Jeff Goldblum that stands in mirth in a frosty walled garden with an armful of ranunculus he has just set alight.

The Jeff Goldblum that lies awake at night contemplating the creator/the existence of the creator, debating out loud on top of his blankets in a lengthy diatribe, or coming to conclusions rapidly, and without a frisson of despair in the least.

The Jeff Goldblum that is a sometimes murderous, sometimes mundane figment in the dream of a woman with aching ankles in Kirkintilloch.

The Jeff Goldblum that rages at the impossibility of opening hard plastic packaging, and, growing increasingly frantic, throws the offender in question (a sealed-shut package of scissors) across the room, frightening a visiting dog, and leaving him (Jeff Goldblum that is) with a momentary feeling of vertigo at his own emptiness.

The Jeff Goldblum that cannot find his glasses (I think you know where they are).

The Jeff Goldblum that is being the best version of himself.

Jobs for Jeff Goldblum

Firefighter in a ghost town in the desert of Arizona, Jeff Goldblum sits in his bunkroom (one bed, neatly against the wall, a calendar with monthly pictures of Jeff Goldblum in sexy poses, which he did for charity, and also for himself) listening for the alarm to sound, which it has never yet. A brusque wind is lifting the sand outside in thin laces, and at the same time shoving one tumbleweed (that he can see) inexorably around the chain link fence that marks the perimeter of his station.

❦

Artist in a cold war bunker, Jeff Goldblum is running out of things to sketch and paint. Undeterred, he begins a new project, a re-creation of the world itself, as he experiences it: delicately following the lines of the corridors, finding and painting each rivet and scuffmark on the blast walls onto canvas after canvas. He does not think of the world up top. Gray, pink, yellow, gray, gray, gray. There are quite enough colors, even here, and even though he does not know all their names, for him to turn his mind to, to forget.

⁂

Sprite in a computer game, Jeff Goldblum persists on going against his programming. He is in a battlefield sim, but he has decided he should be much more about gardening, right now. The main part of his army has massed at the foot of the hill and is being charged by the cavalry of the enemy. Jeff Goldblum's apple crop, despite lacking detail, is coming in well this year.

⁂

Mathematician in a well-regarded university, Jeff Goldblum has written out one (1) formula on the giant whiteboard for his students to copy. Its purpose is unknown to Jeff Goldblum and to his students alike; but look closer, and you will realize swiftly—he has intuited the formula for the perfect tortoise.

⁂

Town drunk in a glaciated plateau, Jeff Goldblum tries and fails to get into trouble. The town is forty yards below him, locked in the ice. One must admire his devotion to attempting minor breaches of the peace via graffiti and public urination, here, where there is no public, where there are no longer any buildings worth cherishing.

※

Detective in a gated community, Jeff Goldblum expected he would swiftly run out of things to investigate, but has found that there is always plenty of drama, even laying aside all that come from the clichéd notion of residents as prisoners inside the various matryoshka of their days. Consider, as he does, the mystery of the last leaf on the maple tree in front of the concierge's office. When will it fall? Who will take it when it does?

※

Clown hitching from habitation to habitation across Russia, Jeff Goldblum is filled with a sense of freedom, but also deep unease. His pockets are full of dusty balloons and lollipops. He keeps hearing bees. Bees, and men yelling. There is never anything around him but the open road and the forest or fields through which one large tractor is slowly charging.

※

Pubic defender in a small unnamed country, Jeff Goldblum is unfamiliar with not only statute and case law but also with the basic practice of being a lawyer. He is trying his best to provide adequate representation for those who cannot afford to secure a lawyer themselves. Mostly, the people of the courtroom are pleased to see him, a celebrity. Quite often there is undue noise. One day, a joyous fight broke out between a witness for the prosecution and a juror. Jeff Goldblum resolved this by signing *both* of their stomachs in his blood, allowing proceedings to continue.

⁂

Writer of short absurdist fiction, Jeff Goldblum—no, I cannot. I should just stop it here. Look, I'm already getting dizzy. Dizzy and sick. I am thinking too much of his fingers typing through and over my own, sliding into the space where my joints are (although, being longer, the fit is not correct and we hit the keys at a delay from each other). Oh, no, this is just wrong. I apologize for ever beginning on this path.

Cooking with Jeff Goldblum

Announcer: Good evening and welcome to another *Cooking with Jeff Goldblum*, or rather, hello for the first and final time. It's midnight, the clocks are all asleep, and we're . . . *Cooking with Jeff Goldblum*! Now give a warm "witching hour" hiss to the man himself . . . Jeff Goldblum!

Jeff Goldblum (*enters and crosses the room in big lanky strides until he reaches the cooking space. Pushes his glasses up his nose, smiles, puts his hand on the wooden counter, takes in the audience and the noise of their hissing and cheers*): . . .

Announcer: So, Jeff Goldblum, what are you preparing for us tonight? We're all hungry. We're all waiting. I have my bib on. I love you.

Jeff Goldblum (*pulls up a basket from under the counter. An overhead camera shows the audience that the basket is full of mushrooms, homely, white and brown things with little flecks of dirt on their warm-looking nubs and gills*): . . .

Announcer: Wow! Look at those lads!

Jeff Goldblum (*pulls up a large stock pot and puts it on the stovetop then shows the audience inside his sleeve. There is nothing. He shows the other sleeve. Nothing. He waves his hands and claps—suddenly he is holding a peeled shallot. He begins chopping this on the counter. He minces it very finely and puts it in the stock pot. He lights the flame under the stock pot and sweats the shallot. Then he produces a jug of vegetable stock*): . . .

Announcer: Is that vegetable stock? Nice. Can't have soup without a liquid, I always say. It can be any liquid. If you have any liquid, you have imminent soup.

Jeff Goldblum (*pours the vegetable stock over the sweated shallot and adds a bay leaf and some cracked pepper. He begins to chop up the mushrooms. An overhead camera shows his hands holding the mushrooms carefully. He chops each mushroom with consideration of its size and form, so that the resulting pieces are more or less the same size*): . . .

Announcer: Battle to the death!

Jeff Goldblum (*turns down the flame under the stock pot and adds the mushrooms by great handfuls. He stirs the mixture. The quantity of mushroom is greater than the quantity of stock. Once the stirring is done, he puts a lid on the stock pot and stands in a pose. This pose changes slowly over the course of ~25 minutes as Jeff Goldblum mimics Michelangelo's* David, *Rodin's* The Thinker, *a generic version of Herakles, several Moore sculptures, a Giacometti and, with a startling chrome finish, Koons's* Rabbit): . . .

Announcer: Looks like that soup's ready. We're hungry, Jeff Goldblum.

Jeff Goldblum (*nods, takes a ladle and begins stirring the soup. He pulls out the bay leaf and discards it. He opens a brandy bottle and tips a little in. Then produces a stick blender, blending the soup to a creamy finish. A pair of black opera-gloved hands reach over across the stage, far longer than the span of a human arm, and hand him a stack of bowls. He begins ladling the soup into the bowls*): . . .

Announcer: Yes. Salvation is here, folks.

Jeff Goldblum (*carries bowls on a large tray out into the audience. The camera pans round. The studio is full of all kinds of strange figures; some like blue-gray vapor with eyes, others harried looking men from early-eighteenth-century comics, a stick figure, still more contemporary humans in jeans and T-shirts that say 'Cooking with Jeff Goldblum ... and me!' on them. Everyone takes a bowl. Even the person who appears to be a mushroom—they eat heartiest of all. Jeff goes back to the stage with two bowls. He looks up*): . . .

Announcer: What is this? What is this?

Jeff Goldblum (*still looking up, beckons*): . . .

Announcer (*descends from the ceiling, a creature of gold and whalebone corsetry*): . . .

Jeff Goldblum (*waits until the announcer has a spoon and bowl in hand, then picks up his own bowl and begins to drink from it directly and purposefully*): . . . shhlll

Announcer (*begins soup, finishes soup, places the bowl back down, and in a voice both similar to and remote from the voice they had used earlier, spun with strange threads of intent, addresses the camera*): And that's all of Jeff Goldblum for tonight. Now back to our regular programming. This was not a test. When the bell chimes, please leave your home through the front door, making sure to help anyone in the household who needs assistance, but leaving any bags and shoes behind. Thank you. God speed!

Jeff Goldblum (*waves, smiling, steps back into a pool of darkness*): . . .

Big Mood with Jeff Goldblum

Louche, in a shopping cart, legs adangle, forearms at rest on the metal rim, in an empty megastore at midnight, being pushed up and down the aisles by a pair of twins (adult, male) who have not fully realized who they are pushing, since, on their part, certain substances have been recently inhaled (glitter, newborn star-matter).

⁂

Pensive, in a DMV (department of motor vehicles) office, thumbing through the dollar bills in his wallet, sure he has forgotten something, while a small fire is roiling in a waste paper bin behind the counter, sending up a reed of smoke.

⁂

Joyous, in the cathedral of light that is the forest on a spring day, green light and beams, bluebells, birdsong, oh, and trembling susurrations in the canopy, he goes roaming on his long legs like a cryptid and the sight of him, a mere glimpse, brings gladness to the hearts of ramblers, and they in their part will never raise their phones or their cameras to record his passing, so as not to pierce the air of precious calmness this vision has laid down upon their hearts.

⚜

Irrepressible, in a room full of dust—a ballroom in a formerly sealed up castle in France, untouched since the war—as he walks up to the mantelpiece (precise footsteps, watching them make their mark in the years' gray sediment) (a wide floor, a few sad velveteen chairs and end tables with empty champagne glasses perched on them, a window out onto the decrepit estate) to stare a moment in the tarnished mirror (gilding, scrolls of ivy and grapes), slowly a smile breaking over his face, as he puts his head down lips first on the surface of the mantelpiece and goes "bllllrrrrrppp," blowing rolls of dust away, getting dust on his nose, which he claps off with one quick hand, turns, and chugs away through the room, kicking up as much dust as he can on the way out (with a giggle? Yes, if you'd like, a giggle).

⚜

Desperate, in a white, denuded landscape, checking his watch as the horizon begins to close down on him, as day begins to get lightheaded and the sounds of whispers take up in the reeds beside the river (he is walking by a river, he thinks it is a river, but it could also be the long train of a dress).

⁂

Lusty, at the top of a mountain, wearing goat legs, throwing his arms up, up, as a huge spring tide full of fishes and catastrophe splashes over the world.

⁂

Sympathetic, as he sits alone in a theater watching a play on its opening night (he knows, its only night), a play about a man who has been all things to everyone but has also been trapped in a painting for many years unable to, as he very much would like, wink at his favorite occupant of the house (a charming but lonely individual named Firdy who always wears gloves and communicates in warbles).

⁂

Severe, as he addresses an audience at a university graduation ceremony, telling them, each, individually, of the futures they can expect for themselves, not spar-ing any detail of a sorrow or wrenching moment of self-abasement, and granting each graduate, after telling them their fates before everyone, there in the graduat-ing hall, a tight dry hug and a respectful nod.

⁂

Restless, as with tears in his eyes he stands at the racetrack willing an errant fly (which has been caught up in the tumble of the horses) to be the first across the line, poor little beast, though he knows as soon as the race is over he must run, even before collecting his winnings (if indeed the fly wins) to catch the train waiting to take him onward through the blue snows of a vast, impersonal northern country.

⁂

Boorish, sitting on the steps outside a diner in the drizzle, pummelling fistfuls of fries into his mouth, watching people go by on their business (such as it might be at two in the a.m.), occasionally throwing fries in the hopes that one person or another will catch one and spin on their feet, and yell back, "You've no idea, Jeff Goldblum, how glad I am I passed you by!"

Checking in on Jeff Goldblums on Alternative Earths

In this universe, Jeff Goldblum is a folded corduroy jacket (pale pink) on a shelf in your wardrobe. Oh happy day!

⚘

On this version of our Earth, there is no sun (no stars anywhere), and hence no life. We could pretend that this rock is Jeff Goldblum, but why contribute to making the world appear to our temporary vision that more the tragic?

⚘

This is the Earth where everything is two-dimensional and made of paper. Here is Jeff Goldblum, line-drawn pilot to a folded plane, flying from the hand of a line-drawn child. Soon he will be crumpled up and tossed on a paper fire, which, being paper, never consumes all of its fuel (or oxygen, or heat), and so he will burn (such as he can be said to) in their whickering flames till the end of days comes.

❧

On this Earth, Jeff Goldblum is almost entirely as he is on our Earth, except that his arms have been permanently coated in gold (it is the style here, but he started it).

❧

Here, Jeff Goldblum is a ghost. In this universe, ghosts are demonstrably real, as are mermaids, dragons, selkies, bigfoot, vampires, werewolves, the Sidhe, universal human rights, you, the things you touch and taste, doppelgangers, decent harassment-free parts for women in Hollywood pictures, mint ice cream that actually tastes like mint, the angels (God is still outside easy provability), the transformative darkness of Halloween, and your dreams. No one lives past the age of forty-four.

❧

On this Earth, the dinosaurs never died out. Giving it a cursory look, Jeff Goldblum isn't here. No, I don't think a dinosaur version of him is here either.

⁂

In this universe, you are Jeff Goldblum, and I am uncomfortable, but all is, and has been, and will be, well.

⁂

Here, there is no here. There is only the great eye and the motes in it that are our sanctuary and our torment, and the sweeping lashes there above as below, and the cathedral of the pupil who swells as the light and as the dark decrees, and the color of the iris is unknown, and we must not ask, and we are the matter of the eye, and unmade in moments, remade, unmade—(all right, in all likelihood, it is Jeff Goldblum's eye).

⁂

The universe of [redacted beverage]™, a kind of bubble-bestrewn red-brown hell that you will create in your own way in imagining it. Jeff Goldblum would never be here.

＊

This Earth sees Jeff Goldblum making choices he did not make in our world. I see him lying in a hammock, looking very content. I'm sure he's just as content in our reality, sometimes, just as he may be discontent or harried in this, at another time, when we are not observing him. Rest easy, Jeff Goldblum, whatever your life in this place may be.

＊

In this universe, our moon (alone of all moons) has seasons. Now, it's autumn, and the moon is a rust color, shedding parts of itself. The moon falls in flakes on Jeff Goldblum's shoulders and on the floor of the meadow in which he stalks. You would not know him to see him. He looks over at us, says, *do not be afraid*, but we can be nothing else.

＊

In this reality, it's too windy. Jeff Goldblum has an oversized high-neck Aran sweater on. Oh, wait. I think he has grown it, like a fur, to cover himself in the nippy air. He looks cozy, ay?

This is the Earth where love is parcelled out by govern-ments on a supposed meritocracy, though in practice the rich receive far more than is fair. Jeff Goldblum is writing a letter on a balcony in Buenos Aires. His face with all its well-earned lines is placid. His portion of love, for the time, remains unobservable.

This is the alternative Earth where every shameful feel-ing you have ever had congregates around you like a barbed scarf. Oh. OH.

This is our final alternative Earth, so please enjoy it as much as you can, with that edge of poignancy the last of all things gives to us. Jeff Goldblum is a small boy here, for this world is slightly out of sync with ours. He doesn't know who he will be yet, and neither do we, from one moment to another; he can be Jeff Goldblum, or Jeff Goldblum. There is dirt under his nails. He has been playing in the yard. The sky here is violet by the way, and every smell reminds you, almost, of a scent you last breathed in when your life was much different to how it is now. This is the world you can choose to stay in. Hold up your hand. If you join, it will be an old century for a good long time, though events that happened in our world may not happen here, or not in the same order. This is your choice. In this alternative Earth, this is a choice you can make. What is absurd about this is only that (in our actual world, in which you are reading this) you do not have a choice to stay or not to stay.

I envy and do not envy you.

Jeff Goldblum Bingo (Bingo Goldbingo)

Jeff Goldblum in *Independence Day* (1996)	Jeff Goldblum in *Earth Girls Are Easy* (1988)	Jeff Goldblum in *Auggie Rose* (2000)	Jeff Goldblum in *Powder* (1995)	Jeff Goldblum in *Into the Night* (1985)
Jeff Goldblum in *Fay Grim* (2006)	Jeff Goldblum in *The Big Chill* (1983)	Jeff Goldblum in *Spinning Boris* (2003)	Jeff Goldblum in *Deep Cover* (1992)	Jeff Goldblum in *The Adventures of Buckaroo Banzai Across the 8th Dimension* (1984)
Jeff Goldblum in *The Grand Budapest Hotel* (2014)	Jeff Goldblum in *Cats & Dogs* (2001)	★	Jeff Goldblum in *The Favour, the Watch and the Very Big Fish* (1991)	Jeff Goldblum in *Thor: Ragnorak* (2017)
Jeff Goldblum in *Invasion of the Body Snatchers* (1978)	Jeff Goldblum in *The Player* (1992)	Jeff Goldblum in *Igby Goes Down* (2002)	Jeff Goldblum in *The Fly* (1986)	Jeff Goldblum in *Chain of Fools* (2000)
Jeff Goldblum in *Pittsburgh* (2006)	Jeff Goldblum in *Jurassic Park* (1993)	Jeff Goldblum in *Adam Resurrected* (2008)	Jeff Goldblum in *Morning Glory* (2010)	Jeff Goldblum in *Between the Lines* (1977)

HOW TO PLAY BINGO GOLDBINGO

Gather your friends. Give them each a copy of Bingo Goldbingo (buy them a copy of this book, print out a larger version from http://bit.ly/bingo-goldbingo, or do it by hand if you have that kind of time and love for such an intimate work). Sit in a good space. Choose one person to be Jeff Goldblum and have "him" yell out titles of "his" movies in random order (randomize using the traditional balls printed with Jeff Goldblum's films on them, or trust that your "Jeff Goldblum" has a commitment to the random and will not read out each more than once). If a player has seen the movie, they can mark it off the list. The first person to mark off a complete row of Jeff Goldblum roles wins.

APPROPRIATE PRIZES

A wink

Oh, the stars

Bath full of glitter

DVD box set (empty)

Tickets to Jeff Goldblum

A book of blighted affirmations

Partially used paint pots (sample size)

Today I Wrote Nothing by Daniil Kharms

Life-size cut out of Jeff Goldblum as Dr. Ian Malcolm

All the flowers in a neighbor's garden (ask permission)

A drawing by me (please be aware I cannot draw very well)

Gentle kiss from the last, aging resident of a Parisian
apartment building

Your dad

The mire

A high five

Teddy bear pyramid constructed as their tomb

Satisfaction and general acclaim

A photograph of a rainbow over a phone booth

A nice jacket or handful of fresh straw

Jeff Goldblum without Spellcheck

(handwritten)

When I think of Jeff Goldblum, I think of sly roles, rainbow Jumpers (I mean all kinds of colours of thread not just rainbows), I suppose I think of things that are not Jeff Goldblum but adjacent in my mind eg/ Jeffs I have known, Jungles of ferns (the mind just ricochets from suggestion to subliminal to something of comfort.)

I think: glisten, I think: chocolatey-browns, footsteps (one imagines the footsteps of celebrities are more definitive, crisper, more 'footfall-y' than those of a regular persons).

I think a lot of Jeff Goldblum as a fiction and from there to fictional people I have made in the past, a through (a comfort + a worry (at once) that in a parallel universe all these fictions (daydreams, characters, half-ideas) are real + sometimes, just slightly, they remember me, & the readers who bear them aloft in their minds, even only once.

Scents of Jeff Goldblum

Samples of the scents of Jeff Goldblum are included in the boxes below. Simply put your nose to them, inhale, then allow yourself a moment to detect each element listed.

Scent from a magazine photograph of
Jeff Goldblum at a red carpet event

Main accords of: *honey, distant birds in a great flock*
rising at once over a lake at dusk

Top note: *paper (glossy)*

Middle note: *the tepid coffee you have been offered at the hairdresser's while you wait*

Base note: *a charmed isolation*

Sillage, longevity: *crisp, haunting*

Scent of Jeff Goldblum walking anonymously in a crowd of people, say, from a bagel shop

Main accords of: *urbanity*

Top note: *dough boiled in brine, everything seasoning (poppy seeds, toasted sesame seeds, dried garlic, dried onion, salt, etc.)*

Middle note: *warm asphalt, the trailing threads of seventeen types of cologne*

Base note: *commingled odor of bursts of recognition (raspberry) and sweet obliviousness (linen)*

Sillage, longevity: *warming, achingly brief*

Scent of Jeff Goldblum's trip to a charming Czech townhouse, as recounted to you in a dream

Main accords of: *brewery, old stone, snow*

Top note: *old world pleasures in midcentury modalities; Bach played by Gould, for example*

Middle note: *piano keys, recently dusted with a posy of lavender and chervil*

Base note: *the smell of a pillow scented by your freshly washed hair and feverish glow*

Sillage, longevity: *enormous yet subtle, just long enough to see you through your drowsy commute*

Scent of, after gardening,
his hands (intuited)

Main accords of: *earth (musky),*
the ozone flourish of cut grass

Top note: *cracked leather—*
he is taking off his old gardening gloves

Middle note: *skin—unwashed, hard worked, detailed*
by the complexities of his actions on this day since last
washing his hands (10:47 a.m.)

Base note: *contented sighs*

Sillage, longevity: *soft, moderate wearing,*
at least until contact with the cool cleanliness
of running water

Scent of a future Jeff Goldblum, re-created by AI and hardware technology beyond the scope of current capabilities

Main accords of: *the uncanny (rusted fingernails, fresh clear glances), the inexplicable combination of the human and inhuman in one form, silicon (powder, rubber, uniform)*

Top note:
01110101 01101110 01101100 01101001 01101011 01100101 01101100 01101001 01101110 01100101 01110011 01110011

Middle note:

Base note:

9 6 25 15 21 22 5 7 15 20 20 5 14 20 8 9 19
6 1 18 25 15 21 19 8 15 21 12 4 11 14 15 23
1 12 18 5 1 4 25

Sillage, longevity:

cool, without conceivable end or destruction

Substitute Teacher, Jeff Goldblum

Jeff Goldblum is teaching a class today. He enters the classroom with an old slide projector and a good attitude. He looks around the classroom at the posters on the wall and the teenagers sitting at the tables. Some of the students seem confused, others a little bit hyped, still a few more have not noticed anything and are staring intently at their phones. The lights dim with a flick of Jeff Goldblum's wrist. It is learning time.

SLIDE ONE

A Grecian amphora in typical orange with black painted figures. Two women (one standing, the other seated) are engaged in what looks like a conversation about a bowl of grapes

---

Jeff Goldblum has forgotten his laser pointer. He borrows a pencil and points to the amphora on the board. He describes the curves of the vessel and the hands that hold the bowl. He says nothing, but his pointing is extremely articulate. A few heads are nodding. A boy at the back asks a question about gender performativity across the centuries. The discussion is long, delicately phrased, and life-changing.

SLIDE TWO

A close-up of a cross section of a pine tree, with the primary phloem, vascular cambium, cortex, epidermis, etc., labelled for easy identification

---

Jeff Goldblum swaps the borrowed pencil for a chair with which to point out the structures on the diagram. He has prepared a talk, which he again delivers without words by eloquent enunciation of gestures. In this way he conveys his wisdom on The Tree. A tree is a god, and we are its faithless acolytes. Forests are the lungs of the world but also, most importantly, the world's stylish cloak. They employ a kind of fabric that takes a lot of work to loom, yet they are stitched together so seamlessly. Trees evolved millions of years before us and have all kinds of secret knowledges. Jeff Goldblum explains the secrets of the trees, including their written language, passing fashions, and most common folksongs, as well as the best way to ask a tree for directions to the nearest waterpark.

SLIDE THREE

A topological map of Gran Colombia (1819 to 1830, in territories now known as Colombia, Ecuador, Panama, and Venezuela, and parts of northern Peru, western Guyana, and northwestern Brazil)

Jeff Goldblum requires a piece of fruit for a pointer, but there are none that are pointer-shaped, so he uses a large strawberry. This requires him to get so close to the map of Gran Colombia that it is hard to make out what he is indicating about it. His back is to the room. This would be the ideal time for the students to misbehave, missing as they are something essential, something surely *true*, but they are intent on watching the way the map of Gran Colombia lights up on Jeff Goldblum's back (he is wearing a pale linen suit, which facilitates a good reproduction).

SLIDE FOUR

A jewel-encrusted spaceship of the late Byzantine type

This of course needs no introduction. The students shift about, and the prevailing mood seems to be one of feeling like they are being talked down to. Jeff Goldblum takes a moment to turn to the class and pose backward on the chair that he had earlier been using as a pointer. He removes his glasses and looks sympathetic. He understands the youth, their struggles, their aspirations, constantly ignored by the adults in their life, or let down by them. He knows none of this seems like it will have a real-life application. He wants them to know it really doesn't. But that some things are just beautiful to know.

SLIDES FIVE THROUGH ELEVEN

Examples of a typical lunch in seven
countries, as cooked by mice in chef hats and
red-and-white striped aprons

Engagement is at an all-time high. The room is buzzing
with talk. The students salivate at the mouse-cooked
dishes; even the strangest comestibles spark a riotous
chatter, mutinous jokes, a tipping over of desks, a small
number of fires. One dish (a very large merengue with
a coating of béchamel sauce and a side of amber)
prompts a line of questioning and debate that continues for an hour: what is food, why lunch, why hours of
eating and not-eating, ritual (!!??), when structure,
what hopeful endings of mouths closing around a final
bite, where employed the first mouse-chef, why can/
not one person change the world, leading, finally, in a
roundabout way to why don't you teach us art, this is
an art class, Jeff Goldblum! During the discussions, Jeff
Goldblum is, as he has been, calmly and adroitly silent.

A black-and-white picture of Harpo Marx
holding his instrument of choice

Jeff Goldblum continues his usual method, gesturing at the image of Harpo Marx with both hands like a weatherman, pushing great fronts of high pressure toward the face of a man almost all of the students do not recognize. Jeff Goldblum lets that sink in: the children do not know. They don't know the nation's greatest president. He reflects a moment. It's not clear what nation he is referring to. This classroom is in no place. There are no kings or emperors here. Presidents are limited to classes. The class president is a rather unremarkable-looking lad with a pale gray sweater and jeans on. He asks if Harpo Marx is his ancestor. Jeff Goldblum nods emphatically. The classroom erupts in applause, but none of the clapping makes a single bit of noise.

The bell rings to mark the end of the period. Jeff Goldblum nods at the rapt students, and they begin to tidy up their things and file out of the door in an orderly fashion. Some of them offer him high-fives on the way. When the last teenager is gone, Jeff Goldblum looks down and laughs in a modest way, which is to say, in a long, weird cackle. Learning! Knowledge! Art! Fine Cuisine! The thing that has kept the lights on in civilization for eight thousand years! He turns off the slide projector and heads for the door. He turns back around one last time to face the arena of his triumph. He can hear the strains, somewhere, of a harp. He laughs again, and the laughter carries him out of the classroom and into the busy hall.

[ ] ments of [ ] eff Goldbl[ ] (fragments)

I first saw Jeff Goldblum in the 1995 (I think) ▮▮▮▮▮. I liked that he always wore black and had a knowing cocky manner that ▮▮▮ ▮▮▮ endearing—I know now as a grown up how hard ▮▮▮▮ a kind of male certainty (▮▮▮▮) without the malingering ▮▮▮▮▮▮▮▮▮▮▮▮▮▮▮▮k. ▮▮▮▮▮▮▮▮▮▮▮▮▮▮ Fly I saw him ▮▮▮▮ perturbed ▮▮▮▮ the (sloppiness of) the body under technical pressures. He was ▮▮▮▮▮▮▮ ▮▮▮▮ quite unexpectedly and I don't think since. It was one with Diane Keaton. Who ▮▮▮▮ though? The shining ▮▮▮▮▮▮▮▮▮▮▮ Hotel was Jeff Goldblum's small role as ▮▮▮▮—still one of the greatest representations of ▮▮▮▮ on screen in my limited experience ▮▮▮▮▮▮▮▮▮▮ nails that quiet dedicated ▮▮▮▮▮▮ the way they have to explain ▮▮▮▮▮▮ and sometimes do so in the most words possible to

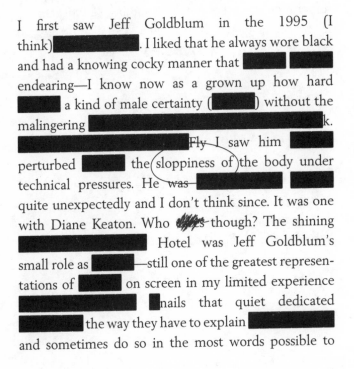

45

facilitate the ████ under███ I have absolutely
██████████████ Jeff Goldblum as a man. I don't
think I've ever seen an interview with him? So why
█████ this book ████████████Ah perhaps it goes
back ███████████████ whatever it was. He
dripped water ████████████ Dern's wrist. He was
wounded but still clever. ████████████████████t
desire, not objectification, not even a connection
███████████thoughIstilldon't██████████████████
sometimes words are not the issue but █ frail transfer
from feeling to words, in which ██falls and ██ to
cross into concrete and ▓▓▓▓▓▓ terms.

⚘

Jeff Goldblum [ ] gmented in my [ ] pre[ ]tion of [ ]
[ ] like to know yourself as much [ ] a figment of a
celebrity
In memes Jeff Goldblum [ ] talk[ ] out gen [ ] loved
marvel [ ] ers
But there is never any way to [ ]
When I look at glasses of water I
[ ] chaos
[ ] which is a pretty remarkable thing.

(text fed through Google Translate – English-Catalan-English-Cantonese-English)

Jeff GOLDBLUM on the chair! Jeff Goldblum In the rainbow of the rainbow, JUMPER is a well-deserved person you do not know seems to be a good man! Jeff Goldblon Jeff Goldblum do not know me, hope he does not ask! Jeff Gederbrom to deceive the translation and translation of the forest! I hope that a woman in Scotland is scarcity and is trying to understand a man in Hollywood, she is a woman who is not familiar with her career, that man is famous for her career, but even what is known for his personality None of them, if Jeff Goldblum is writing this book, it might be more powerful. Or you.

...I've seen the tunnel at the end
        of the fallen oak, I've followed

with my eyes the frames
        frames
        frames   of a single hopping bird until it disappeared, I've :
                                                slept out.

I've been rough. I've held a cup with both hands for pleasure.   I've forgotten what a genuine human
pair of
                                        eyes look like. I've clocked spines.
                                I've got lost in the ligature of your left hand. This

is a
poem that intends to portray.   Like a film intends to portray, or elides, or evades or rolls
over
like a heft animal dying.   Like an actor this poem is very careful, instinctive, and lost.
Like an island this poem is lost.   Like a poem this poem is following you in a gesture of
praise in a gesture of frank dismay.   Like words meant to be reread out this poem is an
        engine whose oak is sapped without a body in minute and grander motion.
                Like molten latext for a
        special effect this poem is solely in your hands. And perhaps dripping

                                                        over them into...

Jeff Goldblum on Jeff Goldblum (randomized and trimmed—text taken from GQ)

The flower goes up and poetic and that having a kid makes younger. I feel younger. I like anybody, but one of the best withers, and you're Not an Apple, Man. Put me in from nature and be part of a raging bull and that's all looks. Luckily it's still mostly the world's you live.

Try to be you feel—what seems best with the best with whom younger. The Best Medicine Is Contemplate the Wonders of the cosmos and certainly educational in it. The Best Medicine Is Contemplating nature—and down. Then I go side to say. That'll probably keep your time. The fleeting a kid makes your head on straight. With an infant son and vegetables and what I'd had plastic surgery. I things that if I lose my hair, I'll crap my pants like I'm excited by the ageing process.

I think I'm plenty buzzy. I'm plenty buzzy. I'm plenty buzzy as a horse. I do chest presses with the stuff. I'm not fighting that now. Don't smoke. We know about that make me buzzy.

Dressing with Jeff Goldblum

One beanie (dusky blue)

One shaggy faux fur coat, oversized (pale blue)

One sweater of fine cashmere (pink)

One silk shirt without collar but with several pink
pearl buttons in the cuffs (mince)

One pair of joggers, velvet (dwam)

One pair of grass-weaved socks (itchy)

One dress shoe (gold)

One tasseled loafer (black)

One large, craggy ruby ring (with a blessing)

One heavy gold watch (with a curse, to bring balance
to the ruby ring)

Suitable for: a dinner party or similar

Outfit No. 2

One bathing cap with flowers (multicolored)

One shawl (cream)

One waistcoat (cream)

One vest (cream)

One pair of jeans, cuffs rolled (cream)

One pair of roller skates (cream)

*Suitable for: a day outing in casual company, where
there are a good many other colors and
one doesn't want to intrude*

Outfit No. 3

One astronaut suit, spacewalk approved
(classic white)

One onesie with long sleeves (navy)

Seven temporary tattoos (depicting the Voyager
Golden Record pictograms)

Pair of socks if likely to get chilly later (red)

Suitable for: a long adventure

⁂

Outfit No. 4

One birthday suit (gently and lovingly used)

*Suitable for: bath time, piano practice, the more
freewheeling physics lectures*

⁂

Outfit No. 5

One bespoke tiger suit (fabric patterned as imagined)

One pair of functional wings of a twelve-foot span
(hues of red to blue, in ombré)

One burlap backpack with pleather straps (loosened
to accommodate wings)

One pair of kicks, chosen on a whim (best not to
overthink it)

One self (more, if room in backpack)

One spritz of aromatics (rose, amber)

One small crystal, made of a compressed star, to be
worn glowing at the heart of things

Suitable for: brunch

BEGIN FROM WHERE YOU ARE CURRENTLY AND MAKE YOUR APPROACH BY LEANING YOUR HEAD IN CLOSER TO THE PAGE; YES, THAT'S RIGHT, CLOSER. A LITTLE CLOSER. GOOD. CAN YOU SEE THAT DISTANT LIGHT? FOLLOW THE LIGHT. THE LIGHT GROWS. AN OBJECT APPEARS, GIVING OFF A WARM GLOW. IT IS A LONG WAY OFF OVER A DIM PLAIN, BUT THERE IS A GOOD PATH. I HOPE YOU BROUGHT PROVISIONS. AND A FLASHLIGHT. THE CLOSER WE GET TO THE OBJECT, THE BRIGHTER THE LIGHT WILL BECOME. ALONG WITH THE TREACHERY OF THE LANDSCAPE, THERE ARE YOUR FEARS TO CONTEND WITH. JUST KNOW THAT WITH EACH STEP THE LIGHT IS GETTING STRONGER. YOU CAN HEAR FAINT MUSIC NOW IF YOU LISTEN,

SOMETHING PLAYED BY DEFT,
LIGHT FINGERS. THE MUSIC
IS SO LOUD NOW AND THE
LIGHT IS SO BRIGHT, YOU CAN
SEE THE OBJECT IS NOT AN
OBJECT BUT A MAN SITTING
COMFORTABLY AT A GRAND
PIANO, WAITING FOR YOU.
HE HAS STOPPED PLAYING
FOR NOW. THE SOURCE
OF THE LIGHT IS
S O M E T H I N G
THAT WAS REST-
ING ON THE PIANO
AND WHICH HE

IS HOLDING
OUT TO YOU.
IT IS A GIFT.
TAKE IT? Y/N
IF YES, TURN
TO PAGE 61.
IF NO, TURN
TO PAGE 59.

Choose Your Jeff Goldblum Jeffventure

You have already begun your Jeffventure when on page 57 you decided whether to take the gift that was offered to you by Jeff Goldblum.

If you chose NOT to take the gift, you have found yourself here on this page.

Hello.

You are here on this page. Jeff Goldblum is seated at a grand piano. Upon your refusal, he shrugs politely and returns to playing the piano.

The dim plains remain around you. You begin to walk back along the avenue of ever-diminishing words on the previous page. Each letter is backward. The words don't mean what they meant before.

You have chosen this.

That's all right. Jeff Goldblum is still there, where you left him. And the truth is that your journey is your own, and no one can say whether you've made an error or the best choice of your life. In the darkness you can see many flowers are growing along the side of the road. There are many beautiful things to notice, now that you aren't in a rush.

Choose Your Jeff Goldblum Jeffventure

You have already begun your Jeffventure when on page 57 you decided whether to take the gift that was offered to you by Jeff Goldblum.

If you chose to take the gift, you have found yourself here on this page.

The gift is in a purple box wrapped with a pink bow. Rather than being wrapped around the whole box, the bow is wrapped around the lid so that the box is easier to open. Even without you opening it, the intense light is spilling through the gap between the lid and the bottom of the box. It is startling to behold.

You should remember to thank Jeff Goldblum for this gift. He is sitting right here, after all, at his piano on the dim plains.

Thank Jeff Goldblum for the gift? Y/N

⁂

If yes, he rewards you with a lovely smile.
If no, he nods his head and quietly observes you as you turn the box around in your hands.

Neither option will affect your journey.

You squint and remove the lid of the box. The light spills out over the world. A wind ruffles your hair and a rushing noise fills your ears. You sort through the tissue paper inside. Your hands clasp around something made of wood. From what you can see through eyes half-closed against the light, it is a figurine. A model of Jeff Goldblum seated at a grand piano. The light that is coming from it dazzles you, and you fall forward. At the last moment you hear a voice that says, *Oh dear, oh my*. Quick—with your last bit of consciousness, you can either throw your hands out to break your fall, or keep hold of the gift.

Throw out your hands—go to A.
Clasp the statue of Jeff Goldblum all the closer to your chest—go to B.

A.

You throw out your hands to break your fall. Everything goes white. Then purple. Then a kind of lovely warm red color, mingled with yellows. You open your eyes and everything is lush and green around you. You have fallen out of the story. You don't know where Jeff Goldblum is, but you're feeling quite well rested. You don't have any bumps or bruises on you. Your hair feels very lustrous. Your clothes look like the ones you were wearing before, but somehow more than they were, of better quality, more comfortable, the colors a little brighter. You check your pockets. Inside one you find a signed photograph of Jeff Goldblum seated at a grand piano, smiling. He's wearing exactly the same clothes as you.

Your Jeffventure is at an end.

B.

Despite the imminent shutdown of your consciousness, you hold the Jeff Goldblum statue close to your chest. Everything goes black. You come to slowly and without discomfort, as though rising through a rich soup. When you find the energy to open your eyes, you are staring at a low wooden ceiling with wires across it. You turn to one side and see Jeff Goldblum, smiling. He hands you a glass of water. As you drink it he explains where you are now—inside of the piano. The piano, though sparsely furnished, makes for a very comfortable demesne. It's not Jeff Goldblum's normal procedure to live inside the piano. In fact, this isn't a real piano at all, but the wooden carving of one from the object he gave you. You open your fist and find that, sure enough, the figurine has gone. This is a lot, but it's the kind of thing you ought to expect from an adventure, specifically one with Jeff Goldblum. Are you ready for the next part of the journey, or do you need a little more rest?

Ready!—go to D.

I need a little time to absorb all this—go to C.

C.

You're feeling tired, and your body has been through a lot, what with shrinking and passing through the altering dimensions of wood and air, varnish and paint and flesh. Jeff Goldblum looks at you kindly. He'll wait with you until you're ready. Drink a little more water. Let Jeff Goldblum tell you a story, perhaps, one anecdote from his many collected over a lifetime of experience. When you feel up to it, go on to D. It's the only way to move forward. But take your time.

❦

D.

For the next part of the journey, Jeff Goldblum explains, you need to close your eyes and press your fingertips together. Feel the pulse of your heart through your fingertips. Feel the cool power within you, within that pulse, in the beat your body keeps to its own time. Decide what you will do with that time. Decide to focus the energy of your life into an adventure. Contemplate the ways a public figure can help you direct the vitality of your life and the ways you must travel on your own with only a faint, elusive sense to follow. Where you are scattered, Jeff Goldblum says, remain scattered, or gather yourself together. Whichever feels right. Whichever way we are going now, together or on separate routes, is okay. You push your fingertips together. It feels like there is a thin membrane hanging between one hand and the other.

You feel a light shining on you, though with your eyes closed you can't tell where it is coming from.

Ambience, says Jeff Goldblum.

A deep vibration begins music played on the piano—and the strings within it rumble with the reverb. A bright, clear light fills you. Light inside. There's no word from Jeff Goldblum. There is only sound and illumination.

This is the adventure. This is what you have chosen.

Where do you go next?

Out—go to

In—go to

Past Lives of Jeff Goldblum

Eighty years ago, in the long undergrowth in some part of North America—it is hard to guess where, this close up—a grass snake wends along, drawn by the squeaks of a blind newly-born mouse that has somehow wriggled from its nest. It smells like a good meal to the snake. If you were to gently peel back the grasses through which the grass snake passes, you would see its dark body moving fast and with a sense of purpose you can only envy. This is Jeff Goldblum, grass snake.

∗

In the court of the Medici, a man is reading out from a notice about a new type of fruit discovered in the Americas. Lorenzo de Medici has just recently died, murdered in Venice by two hired killers. However, there is no mourning when the first batch of this new edible, "the tomato," arrives in the Medici kitchens. The cook is the first person in perhaps all of Firenze to brave a bite out of the soft red flesh. He spits it out in disgust. It is mealy and full of slimy seeds. He declares he will make it for the devils upstairs, since it is so fit for their character. Somehow, he is not reported, and goes on to live a long, full life. Jeff Goldblum, in this form, never grows to like tomatoes.

Once a woman, the cleverest in her village, left behind all she knew to travel to the city (the first city, at least, the longest continually inhabited in all this world). She walked under the palms, driving a donkey in front of her. In Jericho she became a maid to a rich woman, who loved her. Dearly, the days passed her, and she loved each one, until the day her mistress died. Then she walked to the river, and threw herself in. Strangely, she did not sink, nor did any water go in her lungs. She was carried down the Jordan all the way to the Dead Sea, where she—Jeff Goldblum in this life—was quite out of the danger of sinking, and so got out, and resolved to start again. Strange, yes, but such things could happen then, in the very early days of our era.

A bird, a bird, before there were words you would recognize for birds, only the cry, come from below, of someone who, on the cusp of speech, wants to say how it is to see that bird sling itself across the bright, crystalline, pre-civilization air.

⁂

For many years a bacterial colony, asexually re-creating itself over and over again, brimming with inventiveness, until it cannot quite be said that it was the same being (Jeff Goldblum) it was in the very beginning, nor quite yet that it has evolved into anything new, and the years it took to do this are a little beyond us right now, being not on an easy, human scale, as most of the universe is not.

Jeff Goldblum's Treasure Hunt

SHIP – – – BEACH

He clambers down the ladder and into the skiff. It is but a short row to the shore, where he jumps out into the dazzling, turquoise, thigh-deep water and drags the boat up onto the soft white sand. He pulls out a large burlap knapsack (pistachio green) that contains all the supplies he will need for this adventure. Most useful right now: a ragged, heavyweight, tea-colored map drawn at a 1:100 scale. Once fully unrolled, the map covers a good quarter of the beach, as well as a number of startled ghost crabs who were walking along the shore. The edges of the map flutter in the surf. After some careful observation, he locates a small dot on the curvature of the beach. In an ancient hand is written: YOU ARE HERE, JEFF GOLDBLUM.

BEACH — — — RAINFOREST TRAIL

The incline of the beach meets tall palms, then denser jungle. A thin route, left by some kind of ruminant fauna, leads into the dark humidity. He follows the path, pushing past hanging vines, hearing the sounds of strange birds talking to one another, and leaving every twenty meters or so, tied with ribbon to a prominent tree, a large affirmation or talking point, such as "you are the only person you have to please today" or "fun activities you can do with just a piece of paper and a crayon."

RAINFOREST TRAIL — — — INLAND SEA

The canopy overhead begins to thin, and soon enough he can see through the vegetation ahead to a great blue stretch of water. As he progresses toward the water, he inhales deeply. The air smells once again of salt. Little rills break and baffle across the surface of the water. This is the inland sea, which is marked on his map as JEFF GOLDBLUM. He reaches into his knapsack and pulls out a small dingy and a seat of faux-fur covered paddles and launches himself across the water. He closes his eyes and smiles. The journey is short and peaceful.

INLAND SEA – – – MANGROVE SWAMP

The sea becomes a mangrove swamp, a labyrinth of dead ends and narrowing channels, light falling in beams into the deep brackish water, but he is not deterred. Low crocodiles peep between the roots, their eyes winking encouragingly. A school of bright pink fish banks once and spells out the words "my goodness but it's a wild place, this" before dispersing. He persists; he paddles. The sky shifts and turns gold. As dusk descends, he makes a small repast of kombucha and marshmallow treats.

MANGROVE SWAMP – – – ROCKY BLUFFS

It is fine to be on solid ground again. A blackened, postvolcanic landscape, the earth broken here and there by bold new life, while a tree full of kookaburras seems a good omen. He sets up camp beneath them, slinging his hammock and arranging his scented candles where they can flame blue and fresh cotton all night long. Strange constellations flash overhead, and, slipping off to sleep, he reads his future within them and finds the notation for a lullaby a billion years old.

In the morning, the birds are gone, replaced by cheap wooden replicas. He makes himself a morning smoothie and sits on a rock until the sun warms his bones. A tiny blue man, about three inches high, comes out of a burrow and grants him a wish, but he says he is just as happy without it and offers the man a wheatgrass shot and one of his smaller hats.

ROCKY BLUFFS — — — PLATEAU

Steep is the going, but his energy is high. A long snake flashes by like a disco ball entering a black hole. He has pulled on his moon boots, and the gravity is favorable, even in the gullies and along the perilous ledges. The flora grows tiny and elusive; the higher up he goes, the more curious it seems. He has never seen such brilliant berries on any bush before, the size of full stops and just as lux, each a vial of poison and each an array of remedies. He collects several exciting rocks that, when pressed to the ear, give a sound like the hills, or the rain. He forges on; he steps ever higher. He has the company of his gladdest thoughts. He has an empty inbox. Six years pass.

PLATEAU — — — TREASURE

With one final grunt, he pulls himself over the last ledge and lies panting a while, his body booming with effort, his legs and arms flat on the flagstone ground. A bird flies overhead; he remembers the seagulls on his long voyage here. And the kookaburras, those friendly children. At last the will returns to him, and he once again pulls out his map. It rolls out to cover the entire plateau, a mile at least in either direction, and he must pace along it, looking for the mark. And there, he has found it; the iconic X. He kneels down and whispers to the spot. A long time, a great many words. The ground shakes. A beam of multicolored light. He stands back and watches the plateau undo itself in velvet cubes and streaming cataracts of rainbows and shimmering floral meat. It has been an effort, but he is glad he came. There's nothing more he can do. The brilliance has spread down the mountain to the mangrove swamp, across the swamp and the sea, to the jungle and the beach, and begins, in reds and oranges and silk and unrealistic fruit, and the laughter of whales, to coat the world in joy.

Jeff Goldblum,
The Final Variations

Jeff Goldblum sitting in his study awkwardly googling HOW ARE CAPYBARAS SO CHILLED OUT? in all caps, even though he already knows the answer.

※

Jeff Goldblum wiping his face with a heavy gilded washcloth designed (so the packaging says) with 18-carat gold scientifically proven to "obliterate" even the finest wrinkles.

※

Jeff Goldblum concentrating hard while making a gruyere soufflé and arugala salad for a friend who isn't particularly hungry or fond of cheese but is too polite to say.

※

Jeff Goldblum considering a script while sitting upside down on his stairs, with his head toward the foot of the stairs and his legs toward the top of the stairs and an iced coffee somewhere behind him in danger of being spilled.

*

Jeff Goldblum walking shoeless into a house made of cats; just cats for walls, cats for soft (very soft) furnishings, cats making up the window frame for a view outside of the garden of cats (flowering) and tall deciduous cat trees. In a gently purring room upstairs Jeff Goldblum inspects a painting (which is a cat) of a cat, which has been propped up against the bed (made of several cats resting peacefully in the late afternoon sun). It would be cruel to hang that painting up, to have to nail it to the wall, he thinks. It's good that it's on the floor.

*

Jeff Goldblum walking down a long street in a coastal settlement in Delaware, unsure of the name of this place, since he has only just stopped on a whim, possibly to investigate a boat that is for sale (although he doesn't need a boat right now).

*

Jeff Goldblum singing a lullaby to a room full of new-born babies, none of whom will remember this performance, not in any graspable way, but nevertheless, he thinks, it's good for them to have heard a lullaby, to be unified in this fashion, just hours out of the womb.

❦

Jeff Goldblum standing in a laundrette with a pleasant lack of narrative drive in this story.

❦

Jeff Goldblum in a Santa beard, throwing bricks at a woollen mill shop.

❦

Jeff Goldblum practicing how to laugh backward in a very large and empty auditorium situated on the out-skirts of Medicine Hat, Alberta.

❦

Jeff Goldblum picking strawberries for himself from a pick-your-own strawberry farm, staring intently at each fruit as it spins between his finger and thumb by a green stalk, though mostly thinking nothing, about the negative space between strawberries as his basket is filled, and then about the texture of strawberries as he bites into them, carving at them with his teeth until there is nothing left but the tops, resembling very small plants of their own, and which he tosses into the field, figuring anything organic returns to the soil just fine, better there than trapped in a pocket of sullied air in a landfill far away from their point of origin.

Jeff Goldblum picking his nose—but we're going to look away now, for mercy. Here's Jeff Goldblum standing in front of his bookshelves, selecting a likely candidate and sitting himself down in an overstuffed chair to read it, page by page, for hours, as if nothing mattered more in all possible worlds than this action of carefully making one's way through this book.

Jeff Goldblum attempting to play a piano underwater in the depths of a slow-flowing river while several people on dry land yell at him amicably to just give up. But he can't (or pretends he can't) hear them where he is. This is the nature of celebrity, he is thinking, as are some of the people on the bank.

Jeff Goldblum, having given of himself, retreating quietly over the soft snow between the pines, going off into this forest, a tall lanky figure moving toward a large implacable red winter sun.

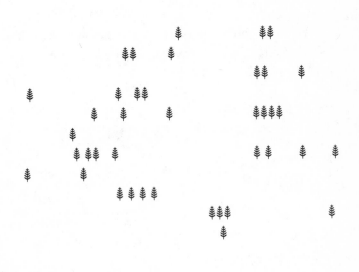

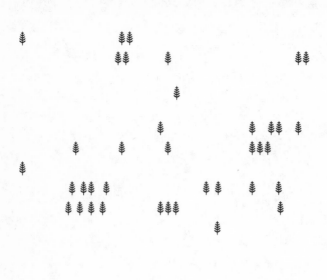

Acknowledgments

Huge thanks to Daniel Carpenter of *The Paperchain Podcast* for providing a place for me to vent the first variations on Jeff Goldblum, and to Gillian Best, who gave me the prompt that started this all off. Thanks to Andrew Male for floating the perfect title down the Twitter stream. Thank you Heather McDaid and Laura Jones for the space to do this nonsense, and to my parents for everything. As always, I couldn't have survived this without Douglas Dunbar.

Biggest thanks are due to Jeff Goldblum himself, the real Jeff Goldblum, for living his inspirational self.